P RESENTS

THE AMERICAN GIRLS COLLECTION®

MEET FELICITY · An American Girl
FELICITY LEARNS A LESSON · A School Story
FELICITY'S SURPRISE · A Christmas Story
HAPPY BIRTHDAY, FELICITY! · A Springtime Story
FELICITY SAVES THE DAY · A Summer Story
CHANGES FOR FELICITY · A Winter Story

1774

MEET KIRSTEN · An American Girl
KIRSTEN LEARNS A LESSON · A School Story
KIRSTEN'S SURPRISE · A Christmas Story
HAPPY BIRTHDAY, KIRSTEN! · A Springtime Story
KIRSTEN SAVES THE DAY · A Summer Story
CHANGES FOR KIRSTEN · A Winter Story

1854

MEET SAMANTHA · An American Girl
SAMANTHA LEARNS A LESSON · A School Story
SAMANTHA'S SURPRISE · A Christmas Story
HAPPY BIRTHDAY, SAMANTHA! · A Springtime Story
SAMANTHA SAVES THE DAY · A Summer Story
CHANGES FOR SAMANTHA · A Winter Story

1904

MEET MOLLY · An American Girl
MOLLY LEARNS A LESSON · A School Story
MOLLY'S SURPRISE · A Christmas Story
HAPPY BIRTHDAY, MOLLY! · A Springtime Story
MOLLY SAVES THE DAY · A Summer Story
CHANGES FOR MOLLY · A Winter Story

1944

FELICITY
SAVES
THE DAY
A SUMMER STORY

BY VALERIE TRIPP

ILLUSTRATIONS DAN ANDREASEN

VIGNETTES LUANN ROBERTS, KEITH SKEEN

PLEASANT COMPANY

The American Girls Collection® is a registered trademark of Pleasant Company.

PICTURE CREDITS
The following individuals and organizations have generously given
permission to reprint illustrations contained in "Looking Back":
pp. 62-63—Copyright © 1984 by The Metropolitan Museum of Art; Colonial Williamsburg
Foundation; pp. 64-65—*Miss Juliana Willoughby*, George Romney, National Gallery of Art,
Washington, Andrew W. Mellon Collection; The Beinecke Rare Book and Manuscript Library,
Yale University (wheelbarrow, watering can, shovel); Dumbarton Oaks, Trustees for Harvard
University (botanical print); pp. 66-67—*The Old Plantation*, Abby Aldrich Rockefeller Folk Art
Center; Reproduced by Courtesy of the Trustees of the British Museum (drum); Collection of the
Maryland Historical Society, Baltimore; North Wind Picture Archives.

Edited by Roberta Johnson
Designed by Myland McRevey and Michael Victor
Art Directed by Kathleen A. Brown

Library of Congress Cataloging-in-Publication Data
Tripp, Valerie, 1951-
Felicity saves the day / by Valerie Tripp ; illustrations Dan
Andreasen ; vignettes Luann Roberts, Keith Skeen.

p. cm. — (The American girls collection)
Summary: During a visit to her grandfather's plantation in Virginia during the
summer of 1775, Felicity's loyalty is torn between her father and Ben, her father's
apprentice who needs her help as he runs away to join George Washington's army of Patriots.
ISBN 1-56247-035-3 — ISBN 1-56247-034-5 (pbk.)
[1. Plantation life—Virginia—Fiction.
2. Virginia—Social life and customs—Colonial period, ca. 1600-1775—Fiction.]
I. Andreasen, Dan, ill. II. Title. III. Series.
PZ7.T7363Fek 1992 [Fic]—dc20 91-44293 CIP AC

TO THE STAFFS OF
PLEASANT COMPANY AND
COLONIAL WILLIAMSBURG
WITH THANKS

TABLE OF CONTENTS

FELICITY'S FAMILY

FATHER
Felicity's father, who owns one of the general stores in Williamsburg.

MOTHER
Felicity's mother, who takes care of her family with love and pride.

FELICITY
A spunky, spritely colonial girl, growing up just before the American Revolution in 1774.

NAN
Felicity's sweet and sensible sister, who is seven years old.

WILLIAM
Felicity's three-year-old brother, who likes mischief and mud puddles.

GRANDFATHER
Felicity's generous grandfather, who understands what is important.

BEN DAVIDSON
A quiet apprentice living with the Merrimans while learning to work in Father's store.

PENNY
The spirited, independent horse Felicity loves.

MR. WENTWORTH
A gentleman who is a neighbor of Grandfather's.

MRS. WENTWORTH
A lady who has strong opinions.

—

KING'S CREEK
PLANTATION

Felicity wanted to whoop for joy. She ran
so fast she was almost flying. Down the
wide stone steps she ran, down the gently
sloping green lawn, and through the garden bright
with flowers. She ran all the way to the edge of the
bluff, and there she stopped.

Below her was the river, wide and blue and
dazzling with light as it flowed along on its way to
the sea. Felicity grinned. Every summer of her life
she had come to stay at Grandfather's plantation on
the York River. And every summer the very first
thing she did when she arrived was run to the river.
Summer did not begin until she'd seen the river's
wide-open sweep and heard its welcoming murmur.

1

Hello, river, Felicity thought. *Here I am, back again. What adventures do you have in store for me this summer?*

Grandfather's plantation was called King's Creek Plantation. It was about halfway between Williamsburg and Yorktown. Corn, wheat, and oats grew in the rolling fields above the riverbank. Cattle, sheep, and horses grazed in the sweet clover pastures. The fields, the slave quarters, and all the outbuildings of the plantation were on either side of the main house. Between the house and the river was a lawn flanked on both sides by dense woods. The lawn was green and broad. It was laced with white shell paths and decorated with flower beds.

Felicity turned from the river and saw her sister Nan and her brother William hurrying toward her along one of the paths. Mother and Grandfather strolled behind at a more gracious pace. Mother's parasol floated like a butterfly above the colorful flowers.

"Lissie," said Nan as she and William reached the riverbank, "I've brought your gathering basket. Grandfather says the first blackberries are ready to pick."

Felicity turned from the river and saw her sister Nan and her brother
William hurrying toward her along one of the paths.

"Blackberries!" said William, all out of breath. "I'll eat the most!"

"Aye!" laughed Felicity. "And you shall most likely eat them before they're ever in your basket!"

"Felicity, do you remember where the best blackberry bushes are?" asked Grandfather with a twinkle in his eye.

"Indeed I do!" said Felicity. "They're in the thicket at the edge of the woods."

"Quite right," said Grandfather.

Felicity smiled at him. "You know I remember everything about King's Creek Plantation, Grandfather," she said.

"I believe you love it as much as I do," said Grandfather proudly.

Mother slipped her hand through the crook of Grandfather's elbow. "Off with you then, children," she said cheerfully. "Your grandfather and I will wait in the shade by the house while you gather blackberries for us."

Felicity grinned at Nan and William. "Let's race!" she said. The three children set off at a run toward the berry bushes.

"That's my Lissie," laughed Mother to Grand-father. "She's not here an hour and already she's running as wild as one of your colts!"

The bushes were thick with berries. In no time at all, Nan and Felicity had filled their baskets. William's basket was only half full, but he himself was covered with berry juice as dark as ink.

After the children washed their hands, they presented the berries to Grandfather and Mother. "Thank you!" said Grandfather. He popped a berry into his mouth. "These blackberries are fit for the king!"

"We have something else for you, too, Grandfather," said Felicity. She handed him a package. "It is a gift from Father's store." Mr. Merriman had stayed in Williamsburg to run his store with Ben, his apprentice, to help him.

"Father let me choose it," said William. He watched impatiently as Grandfather unwrapped the package. "It's a bird bottle," William explained. "You put it on the side of a building, and birds build nests in it and eat any insects that come around."

bird bottle

5

"How very fine!" said Grandfather. "I thank you."

"Of course, birds build their nests in the spring, not the summer," said Nan in her sweetly serious voice. "There's no sense in putting up the bird bottle now. 'Tis the middle of July."

Felicity saw William's disappointed face. "Oh, but the birds will surely want to *visit* the bird bottle," she said quickly. "I think we should put it up right away. Don't you, Grandfather?"

"Yes, indeed," said Grandfather. And so the three children helped Grandfather attach the bird bottle to the smokehouse, just under the eave of the roof.

When they were finished, Grandfather said, "There! Now perhaps I will have birds as well as children visiting this summer." He put his arm around Felicity's shoulders and smiled down at her. "All my visitors make me very happy."

That evening, while Nan, William, and Felicity were playing battledore and shuttlecock on the lawn, they saw a bird fluttering around the bird bottle. They stood quietly. The bird perched on the bottle, tilted his

battledore

shuttlecock

head, and studied them with his bright black eyes. He chirped mightily for a while, as if to proclaim his ownership of the bird bottle. Then he flew away.

"Why didn't he go inside the bird bottle?" asked William.

"He's probably too busy," Felicity answered. "He doesn't want to be indoors, anyway. There's too much to do out of doors."

That was certainly how Felicity felt. She loved summers at Grandfather's plantation because she could be out of doors almost all day long. It seemed to her that life on the plantation was busy and lazy at the same time. There were a great many things to do, all of them pleasant, and there was never any hurry about getting them done.

Felicity's days began early and peacefully. Every morning before dawn, Felicity and Grand-father met at the stable. Grandfather rode his old stallion, Major, and Felicity sat sidesaddle on a ladylike mare named Jessamine. Together they rode at an easy trot to the bluff above the river. There they waited for the sunrise.

The early morning was so still, Felicity thought she could almost hear the sun rising. It seemed to whisper as it slid smoothly up from behind the hills, warming the gray clouds to pink, the black hills to green, and the silvery river to blue. The sun filled the day with light and color.

"Well, now, Felicity my dear," Grandfather would say as they felt the sun on their faces, "let us put this day to good use." And they would gather their reins and turn their horses toward the fields.

Some mornings Felicity and Grandfather rode from one end of the plantation to the other, all the way from King's Creek to the old footpath that led to Yorktown. There was so much to see! Summer was a generous season. Strawberries grew in thick clusters along the edges of the fields. Fat watermelons and muskmelons grew in the melon patch. Plump peaches, nectarines, and figs grew in the orchard, just waiting to be plucked and eaten. Lavender grew in the sunny herb garden. The air was sweet with the smell of sun on flowers and fruit.

While the morning was still cool, Felicity and Grandfather inspected the green fields. She'd listen while Grandfather spoke to the field hands and the overseer about the weather. She'd let go of the reins

while Jessamine grazed with the sheep and cows in the grassy meadows.

Most of all, Felicity loved to watch the horses running in the huge, fenced pasture. Grandfather loved horses, too. He understood how Felicity felt when she talked about Penny, the horse she had secretly tamed and then had helped run away from its cruel owner, Mr. Nye. "Whenever I see horses, I search for Penny," Felicity said. "I never have stopped hoping that someday I will see Penny again. Do you think that's being foolish, Grandfather?"

"No, my dear girl," said Grandfather. "I think that's being faithful."

When the morning grew warmer, Grandfather and Felicity would head back to the house through the woods. Grandfather would often stop to point out and name the wild herbs and other plants they passed.

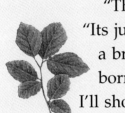

"That's witch hazel," he said one day. "Its juice makes a good medicine to put on a bruise. If you gather some sprigs, we'll borrow the cook's mortar and pestle and I'll show you how to grind witch hazel to extract its juice."

witch hazel

Felicity slipped down from her saddle to pick sprigs of witch hazel and put them in her gathering basket.

One morning, Grandfather told Felicity about the times when he was a young man who had just arrived in Virginia from England. "I often went west on hunting trips," he said. "I lived alone in woods like these for days."

"But where did you sleep?" asked Felicity. "What did you eat?"

"Fallen trees gave me shelter. Pine boughs were

my bed," answered Grandfather. "I hunted birds and game. I ate roots and berries. 'Twas a fine, simple life."

"It sounds so adventurous!" said Felicity. She imagined living in the cool, dark woods, under a fallen tree, where she would be surrounded by the smell of rich, damp earth. How wonderful to be so wild and free!

"The earth is happy to provide us with everything we need," said Grandfather as they left their horses at the stable. "We must only be wise enough to know how to use it."

FAITHFUL FRIENDS

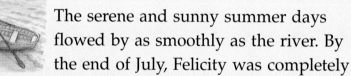

The serene and sunny summer days
flowed by as smoothly as the river. By
the end of July, Felicity was completely
settled into the rhythm of life on the plantation.
She often thought of her father, and Ben, and her
dear friend Elizabeth back home in Williamsburg.
She missed them not because she was lonely, but
because she wanted to share with them all the
good times and quiet delights of summer at King's
Creek Plantation.

One hot afternoon, Felicity and William were
playing by the river in Grandfather's boat, which
was pulled partway onto the shore. William was
pretending to row. The family had rowed upriver to

a barbecue and boat race the day before, and
William was now determined to be a boatman.
Felicity had a shell full of soapy water. She dipped
a hollow reed in it and blew bubbles, and then
watched the bubbles drift lazily up toward
the clouds.

The sun was as heavy as a weight
on Felicity's back. But she had taken
off her shoes and stockings so that
she could dangle her legs over the
end of the boat and dip her toes into
the river water. And her wide-brimmed straw
hat shaded her face, so Felicity felt perfectly
comfortable.

Nan appeared at the top of the bluff. She
waved and called out as she ran down to them,
"Lissie! William! 'Tis time for dinner."

William quickly climbed out of the boat. He
was always interested in dinner. But Felicity sighed
as she pulled her feet out of the water. She was
always sorry to go inside.

"Lissie!" giggled Nan when she got to the boat.
"Gracious me! Hurry and put on your shoes and
stockings. Mr. and Mrs. Wentworth are here to visit.

It wouldn't be proper for guests to see you bare-legged!"

Felicity sighed again as she put on her shoes and stockings. "I wish we had no guests today," she said. "I'd rather stay out of doors."

There were very often guests for dinner. Ladies and gentlemen from all the neighboring plantations came to call on Mother. She had grown up here on Grandfather's plantation, and all her old friends were eager to see her. Felicity liked it very much when families with children visited. All the children had dinner by themselves, separately from the  adults. They ate their dinner quickly and then were free to go out of doors. They went for walks or played battledore and shuttlecock on the lawn. But when there were no children visiting, Felicity ate with the adults. Nan and William ate in the kitchen. It was considered a privilege to be allowed to join the adults in the dining room. But it did not feel like a privilege when Mrs. Wentworth was one of the dinner guests. Felicity feared it would be a dull afternoon.

And indeed, Mrs. Wentworth had a great deal to say at dinnertime. "Well!" she exclaimed. "When I heard that Governor Dunmore and his family had left Williamsburg, I quite nearly went into spasms! Governor Dunmore was sent to the colonies by the king himself to govern us. If he must flee from his Palace, then none of us is safe! We shall all be murdered in our beds by these wild Patriots! They are disloyal to our king!" She turned to her husband, who appeared to be dozing. "Don't you agree, Mr. Wentworth?" she asked sharply.

"What? Oh! Yes, indeed, my dear," said Mr. Wentworth.

"Think of it!" Mrs. Wentworth went on. "The governor and his family were forced to stay on a ship in Norfolk! I hear Lady Dunmore and the children are now sailing safely home to England. Well!" Mrs. Wentworth's plumpish face was pink as a boiled ham. "I'm simply scandalized! I'm glad you're far from Williamsburg this summer, my dear Mrs. Merriman. And your dear sweet children! Do you not fear for your husband? And you in your condition, too!"

Felicity saw her mother blush. Mother was

expecting a baby in the winter. "My dear Mrs. Wentworth," Mother said calmly, "do not upset yourself. 'Tis true, the governor and his family left Williamsburg. Relations between the governor and the colonists were no longer friendly. But 'twas a peaceful departure. No one wished the governor or his family any harm. As for my husband . . ." Mother smiled. "I've no fear for him. He is a sensible, peaceful man. He keeps a cool head."

Mrs. Wentworth waggled *her* head. "Well!" she

went on. "All this trouble began in November, when those hot-headed Patriots threw crates of tea into this very river, just down the

crates of tea   road in Yorktown. 'Twas then that so many merchants decided to stop selling tea in their shops. They stopped because they were too disloyal to pay the king's tax on it! Scandalous, if you ask me."

No one *had* asked Mrs. Wentworth. In fact, no one had said anything at all. Felicity, Mother, and Grandfather were awkwardly silent because Felicity's father was one of the merchants who had stopped selling tea in his store. He had stopped because he believed the king's tax was unfair, not because he was disloyal.

Felicity glanced at Grandfather. She knew he thought Father was wrong not to sell tea. But Grandfather was too polite to say anything that would make Mother uncomfortable in front of the Wentworths. *'Tis a good thing Ben is not here,* Felicity thought. Ben was a Patriot, heart and soul. He'd be sure to say something that would send Mrs. Wentworth into spasms.

The dining room was hot and stuffy, and Mrs. Wentworth's words only made it worse. Felicity knew she should sit still and appear to be interested in the conversation even though she did not like what Mrs. Wentworth was saying. But her feet were jumpy, and her legs itched. There was sand stuck in her stockings. Felicity put her hands through the slits in her gown and petticoat as if she were reaching into her pockets. She slipped her hands past her pockets, untied her garters, and put them in her pockets. Then she jiggled her legs so that her stockings fell down around her ankles. Ah, now, *that* felt better!

"Gracious!" said Mrs. Wentworth suddenly.

Felicity realized Mrs. Wentworth was looking at her.

"Felicity!" Mrs. Wentworth puffed. "You are as twitchy as a cat's tail! What ails you, child?"

Quickly, Felicity put her hands up on the table. "Well, I . . ." she began.

Grandfather rescued her. "May I ask you ladies to excuse the gentlemen?" he asked. "Mr. Wentworth has brought some horses for me to look at. And I would like Felicity to join us. I shall need her advice. She has quite an eye for a good horse."

"Oh, yes, of course!" said Mother. Mrs. Wentworth nodded.

Felicity was so grateful to be going, she forgot about her stockings. They flopped around her ankles as she followed the gentlemen out of doors and down the path to the pasture behind the stable. The sun was scorching hot. Still, it felt wonderful to be out of doors.

Felicity took a deep breath. She loved the stable smell of horses and sun-warmed hay. She stood next to Grandfather and looked over the pasture fence at the five horses Mr. Wentworth had brought. Most of the horses stood quietly in the

"Felicity!" Mrs. Wentworth puffed. "You are as twitchy as a cat's tail! What ails you, child?"

shade of the stable, nibbling at the
grass. Felicity shaded her eyes to
better see one horse that was at
the far end of the pasture, trotting
restlessly along the fence.

"These are cart horses," Mr.
Wentworth said to Grandfather. "Some of them
are handsome enough to pull your riding chair.
The others are steady and strong. You won't
find a better horse than one of these to pull a
farm wagon."

"They appear to be in fine condition," said
Grandfather. "Let's have a closer look." He opened
the gate and led Felicity and Mr. Wentworth into
the pasture. The stable boys looped ropes around
the horses' necks and led them to Grandfather
one by one. Grandfather inspected the horses
carefully. He ran his hands down their legs and
looked at their eyes and teeth to be sure the
horses were healthy.

Suddenly, there was an uproar. The horse at the
far end of the pasture whinnied, and kicked up its
heels, and ran wildly. It would not let the stable
boy near enough to put the rope around its neck.

Mr. Wentworth shook his head. "That horse was passed along to me in a swap and I took her, for she's a thoroughbred," he said. "She's handsome, and fast as the very wind. But she's very skittish. I fear she was once so badly mistreated, she trusts no one."

The horse reared up, and Felicity gasped. She slipped past Grandfather and ran toward the horse as fast as she could.

"Stop!" Mr. Wentworth shouted. "Stop! That horse is dangerous!"

The horse was skinny and scruffy and so covered with dust that her coat was the color of mud. She tossed her head and danced from side to side. Felicity made herself slow to a walk as she came nearer. Her heart thudded in her chest so that she could hardly breathe.

"Penny," Felicity said softly. "Penny. It's me. It's Felicity. You remember. You remember me, don't you, Penny? Don't you, my girl?" Felicity stood still and held out her hands. "Come to me, Penny," she said. "Come, my fine one."

The horse nickered. She took one step, then two, toward Felicity. Then, very gently, she nudged

Felicity's shoulder with her nose.

Felicity's eyes filled with happy tears. She reached up and put her arms around Penny's neck. "I knew we would find each other again someday," Felicity whispered.

Felicity turned and slowly walked back toward Grandfather. Penny followed close behind her. The men stood by the stable, watching, silent. Felicity smiled at Grandfather. "This is my horse, Grandfather," Felicity said simply. "This is Penny."

Grandfather's gray eyes shone with happiness. He cleared his throat. Then he said to Mr. Wentworth, "I'll take this horse along with the others, if you'd be so kind." He shook hands with Mr. Wentworth to seal the bargain.

"I've never seen such a thing in all my days," said Mr. Wentworth. "It does my heart good to know that horse has found a home." He turned to Felicity. "You're a brave young lady," he said. "You deserve a horse as spirited as this."

"She does indeed," said Grandfather. "She does indeed."

That night, Felicity took paper from the leather pocketbook Father had given her. She wrote a letter to Father and Ben to tell them about Penny. She knew Ben would be happy, because he had shared her secret about taming Penny last autumn. That had been the beginning of her friendship with Ben.

Then Felicity wrote:

30 July, 1775
My Dear Friend Elizabeth,
I pray this Letter finds you in good Health and good Spirits. Such great Happiness is mine! Today, my dear horse Penny is returned to me. Grandfather has purchased her. I am to care for her while I am here. All

this afternoon I have spent with her, brushing and currying her. She is thin, but in good Health. My Joy is twice as great, because I know you share it with me. You hoped for Penny's return as much as I did, and never let me lose Faith. Tonight my Heart is full of Happiness, and full of Love for you. I am, and shall be forever,
    Your faithful Friend,
    Felicity Merriman

CHAPTER
THREE

THE NOTE IN THE BIRD BOTTLE

During the months they had been apart,
Felicity had often imagined what it would
be like if she were ever with Penny again.
But even in her dreams, she had not imagined how
happy she would feel, or how content. It was as if
something sad and longing in her had finally come
to peace, all because Penny was back.

"I have never seen two living creatures so glad
to be with one another," said Grandfather. He and
Mother were watching Felicity make medicine to
put on a scrape on Penny's leg.

"Aye," agreed Mother. "Indeed, 'tis a pleasure
to see."

Felicity ground herbs with the pestle to make a

smooth mixture. Then she scooped up some with her fingers and spread it on Penny's scrape. "The wound is healing well, Grandfather," she said.

"You have done a fine job of caring for that horse," said Grandfather. "She looks like a different animal entirely from the wild creature that she was two weeks ago. She's filled out, and her coat is as shiny as a . . ."

"Bright copper penny!" Felicity said. "Isn't Penny a love, Grandfather? She's so fast! And did you see how well she accepted the sidesaddle? She took to it better than I did myself!"

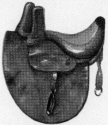

sidesaddle

"You do look like a fine lady upon her, Lissie, my dear," said Mother. "I wish your friend Elizabeth could see you. She would be so happy."

Felicity felt a tiny prick of sorrow. Elizabeth had sent her a lovely letter saying how happy she was that Penny was with Felicity again. But Felicity did not know if Elizabeth would ever see her with Penny. Penny was to stay on Grandfather's plantation when Mother and the children returned to Williamsburg at the end of August. After all,

Grandfather owned her. Besides, if Felicity brought
Penny back to Williamsburg, it might be dangerous.
There was no telling what Mr. Nye would do. He
was the man who had claimed to own Penny last
fall. He had beaten and starved her. He might steal
Penny away and hurt her again.

But for now, Mr. Nye was far away, and Felicity
spent every minute she could with her beloved
horse. When she and Grandfather rode in the
mornings, Penny was well behaved. She followed
Grandfather's horse obediently and never fought
the slow, steady pace. Their morning rides were
such a pleasure, Felicity and Grandfather made
them longer. Sometimes they followed the footpath
as far as Philgate's Creek. Once, they even crossed
the creek and rode all the way to where the path
split. One fork led to a little finger of land that
stuck out into the river, called Sandy Point. The
other fork led to Yorktown.

After dinner, when Nan and William played
and Grandfather and Mother rested, Felicity rode
Penny to the huge upper pasture. The grass seemed
to shimmer with heat, and the air was so dense and
hot it felt solid. Felicity would lean forward and

whisper, "Run, Penny, as fast as you like." Penny would walk, then trot, then canter. Faster and faster Penny would fly, smooth as water, while Felicity held on tight, and the whole world was a brilliant blur around them.

One steamy afternoon, as Felicity was riding Penny from the stable to the upper pasture for their canter, she passed Nan and William. They had reeds, and shells full of soapy water, and they were blowing bubbles up into the branches of a large, old shade tree.

"Lissie," said William, "when you pass the bird bottle, do remember to look inside it. Maybe a bird has built a nest today."

Felicity and Nan looked at each other and sighed. William asked Felicity to look in the bird bottle almost every day, even though both girls had told him a hundred times that birds don't build nests in the summer. "William," said Nan patiently, "you and Lissie looked yesterday. There is no nest in the bottle. There never is. There never is *anything* in the bottle."

William ignored Nan. "You'll look, won't you,

Lissie? Promise?"

"I promise," said Felicity quickly. She was impatient to go. She nudged Penny, and they trotted away. As they passed the smokehouse, Felicity glanced at the bird bottle to keep her promise to William, even though she knew nothing would be there.

But to her great surprise, Felicity saw something white in the bird bottle. She reined Penny to a stop and squinted at it. Was the sun playing tricks on her eyes? Felicity rode up for a closer look.

There *was* something there. It was a scrap of cloth. Felicity put her hand in the bird bottle and pulled the cloth out. It looked like the corner of a handkerchief. It was wrapped around something hard, something like a stick. Quickly, Felicity unrolled the cloth. Out fell a wooden whistle. Felicity stared at it. She knew it was a signal whistle because she had seen Ben's. He had shown her how to blow it, and how it was used to give commands to soldiers. In fact, this signal whistle looked exactly like Ben's. Whose was it? Why had someone put it in the bird bottle? Why was it wrapped in a scrap of handkerchief that was stained with berry juice?

Felicity looked at the stains more closely and gasped. They were not stains at all! They were words, written with a stick dipped in berry juice! Felicity read the words on the scrap of cloth:

Ben? Ben was supposed to be in Williamsburg. How could he have left this note for her? Where was he? If he was nearby, why didn't he come to the house? And why did he need her help? Felicity's mind was spinning.

Below the words on the scrap of cloth, Ben had made a rough map. The map showed Grandfather's house, the river, and the woods. There was an X in the woods. That must be where Ben was.

Felicity took a shaky breath. Suddenly, it was all clear to her. Ben was hiding. For some reason, he didn't want anyone but her to know where he was. Ben wanted her to find him by following the map. She should blow his signal whistle so that he would know it was safe to show himself. Felicity did not stop to think anymore. She urged Penny to a trot and went to look for Ben in the woods.

Felicity and Penny entered the woods just behind the blackberry thicket. When they were deep in the forest, Felicity blew the signal whistle once, twice, three times. She heard Ben whistle in reply, and she rode toward the sound. It was not hard to find him, though he was well away from the riding path. He sat propped up against a big tree. One leg was stretched out in front of him, wrapped in bloody rags.

"Ben!" exclaimed Felicity. "Benjamin Davidson! What on earth are you doing here?" She slipped off Penny's back. "What's happened to you?"

Ben groaned and closed his eyes. Felicity stopped talking. She knelt next to him and then said quietly, "Ben, tell me what you are doing."

Ben opened his eyes. His face was sweaty and streaked with mud. "I ran away," he said. "You know I want to be a soldier and fight with the

"Benjamin Davidson! What on earth are you doing here?"

Patriots. Two companies of soldiers from Virginia have already marched to Massachusetts to join the army George Washington is gathering there." Ben took a deep breath. "It's starting, Lissie," he said. "General Washington is going to lead an army of Patriots. We're going to fight the British. We're going to overthrow the rule of the king here in the colonies. I want to be part of the fight. But my apprenticeship agreement with your father won't allow it. So," he repeated, "I ran away."

"When?" asked Felicity.

"The night before last," answered Ben. "I thought I could make it to the Yorktown ferry and cross the river before your father . . . before I was missed."

Felicity sighed. "What went wrong?" she asked.

"I knew I couldn't walk along the main road for fear of being seen," said Ben. "Still, I made good time through the woods until I came to King's Creek. It was so dark, I slipped and fell when I was crossing the creek. I lost my pack of clothes and food and money. And I cut my leg on a sharp branch."

"Your leg looks bad," said Felicity. "It must hurt."

Ben shrugged. "I knew I was not far from your Grandfather's plantation, and I knew I needed your help. I found my way here and slept by this tree. Yesterday, I sneaked up closer to the house. I saw you and William looking at the bird bottle. So last night, I wrote you that message and hid it with my whistle in the bird bottle. I was hoping you'd find them today. I am very glad you did."

"I'm glad, too," said Felicity. She stood up and dusted off her gown. "Because now I can tell you how foolish I think you're being. I'm going straight up to the house to fetch Grandfather."

Ben reached up and grabbed Felicity's arm. "Don't!" he said. "Your grandfather is a Loyalist. He thinks the Patriots are wrong. You can't tell him about me, Lissie!"

Felicity jerked her arm away. "Yes, I can!" she said. "I'd be dishonest if I didn't. I can't keep a secret like this!" She stalked away and swung herself up onto Penny.

"Lissie," said Ben softly, "that's Penny, isn't it? I got your letter, saying that she was here. You must be happy to have your horse back."

"Yes!" said Felicity, "I—" Suddenly, she stopped. She looked down at Ben. He was solemn. Felicity remembered how Ben had helped her keep Penny a secret last fall. Ben had never told Mother or Father that Felicity was sneaking off every morning to ride Penny. She had asked Ben to keep her secret, and he had. How could she not do the same for him?

Felicity spoke slowly. "Very well, Ben," she said. "I promise I will not tell anyone about you. You can trust me. I'll go back to the house now. But I'll be back soon with food and water and some medicine for your leg. Rest easy. I won't be long." She smiled at Ben a little bit. "You kept my secret. I shall keep yours. I promise."

Ben grinned for the first time. "I knew you would, Felicity," he said. "You are a faithful friend."

CHAPTER
FOUR
—

RUNAWAY

 The afternoon sun was shining strong on the pines, and the air was scented with piney tang when Felicity returned to Ben in the woods. She handed Ben a basket of food. "You look as though you need this," she said.

Ben took the food gratefully. "Indeed I do!" he said. "I've eaten enough blackberries to fill twenty pies, but I am still hungry!"

"You'll need your strength," said Felicity. She knelt next to him. "I'm going to look at your leg." Very gently, Felicity unwrapped the rags from around Ben's leg. They were stiff with dried blood. Underneath them, Felicity saw a jagged gash running from the ankle to the knee. She washed the cut with river water she'd brought. "Now I'm going to put medicine on your leg," she told Ben. "It may hurt a bit."

Ben concentrated on the bread he was eating. He only flinched a bit at the medicine's sting. "How do you know so much about medicine?" he asked.

"Grandfather taught me," said Felicity. "He showed me how to grind herbs to make this medicine for Penny. It helped her scrape heal. It should help you, too."

Felicity wrapped Ben's leg in strips from a clean petticoat. She tied the bandage around his leg with a ribbon.

Ben smiled when he looked at the ribbon. "Well," he said, "my leg certainly looks prettier. It feels better, too."

"It will be as good as new in a week or so," said Felicity.

"A week!" exclaimed Ben. "I can't wait here that long!"

Felicity shrugged. "You have no choice.

Besides," she said briskly, "I can't see that a sickly, skinny, limping soldier would do General Washington and his army one bit of good." She stood up and began to gather pine boughs from a fallen tree to make a bed for Ben.

"Felicity," said Ben. "What do you think about all this—about General Washington and his army of Patriots?"

"I'm sorry the disagreements between the king and the colonists have gone so far," said Felicity. "I hoped there wouldn't be any fighting. I hoped the differences could be solved another way."

"That's what your father says," said Ben. "So you agree with him. You think I am wrong."

Felicity sat down and looked straight at Ben. "Aye," she said. "I can't say you are wrong to stand up for what you believe in. But I do think you are going about it the wrong way. Breaking your apprenticeship agreement with my father is not honorable. It's wrong the way a lie is wrong. You'll shame your family and yourself. I'm afraid—"

"*I'm* not afraid," Ben cut in. "If you were older, you'd understand."

"Oh!" said Felicity tartly. "Well! I understand enough to know that this is not a brave beginning! If you run away from my father, what will happen when you meet an enemy?"

Ben was quiet.

"Did you even talk to my father?" Felicity asked. "Did you even ask him to let you go?"

Ben frowned. "You know as well as I do that he would hold me to my apprenticeship agreement," he said. "Your father would not let me break my promise to him."

"Indeed," said Felicity slowly. "I always thought it was a promise you made to yourself, to do what you said you would do, no matter how hard it was."

Ben leaned his head back against the tree.

Felicity stood up. "I'm going now," she said. "But I will be back tomorrow. I hope you'll think about what we've said."

"I will," said Ben. "But I will not change my mind."

"No," said Felicity, "but maybe you will have a change of heart."

It was not difficult for Felicity to visit Ben the next few days, nor was it difficult to find food for him. The cook never minded if Felicity took food from the kitchen, and it was easy to gather berries and peaches still warm from the sun. Felicity put to use some of the things Grandfather had taught her about living in the woods to make Ben more comfortable. The medicine was helping Ben's leg heal quickly. In fact, Felicity did not want to tell Ben how well his leg was healing. She kept hoping he might decide not to go. But the decision was forced upon him sooner than she expected.

One morning, as Felicity, Nan, William, and Grandfather were eating their breakfast, Mother came into the dining room and handed Grandfather a letter. Then she turned to the children and said, "The letter is from your father, children. He is coming here tomorrow, rather than waiting until Sunday as usual."

"Hurray!" said Nan and William.

Felicity wished she could feel as happy as

they did. But she couldn't. She thought she knew why Father was coming. He was looking for Ben. She made her voice sound calm. "Oh! How fine," she said.

Grandfather put the letter down and said crisply, "It seems that Ben, that hot-headed apprentice, has run off. I warned your father about Ben when I was in Williamsburg this spring. I said he was spending too much time watching the militia muster. Now it appears I was right. That foolish boy has run off—probably to fight with the Patriots. Humph! Your father is well rid of such a troublesome scoundrel."

"Now, now," said Mother. "Ben's a good lad. Maybe he's gone to visit his family and plans to come back."

"Well!" said Grandfather. "Then why did he leave without a word? And why did your husband put a notice in the *Gazette?*"

"Father put a notice in the newspaper?" asked Felicity.

"Aye," said Grandfather. "Here it is. You may have it."

Felicity's eyes widened with fear as she read:

> **WILLIAMSBURG,** *August* 19, 1775.
>
> **R**UN away from the Subscriber, on the 15th Day of *August*, an APPRENTICE Lad named BENJAMIN DAVIDSON, 6 feet high, about 16 years old, slender and well made, of a clear complexion, has long brown hair, brown eyes, a forthright look, and frank manner. I have reason to believe he is headed *Yorktown* way. Whoever delivers the said Apprentice to me shall have eight dollars Reward; and I hereby forewarn all persons not to harbour or entertain him.
>
> EDWARD MERRIMAN.

Felicity excused herself and hurried to her bedchamber. She sat at the open window and looked out across the long lawn. She could see the river flowing along to the sea. It never stopped. It never wavered. The river was always so sure of its course. But Felicity was not. She did not know what to do. She looked down at the notice in her hand. "I hereby forewarn all persons not to harbour or entertain him," Father had written. By caring for Ben and helping him hide, Felicity was doing exactly what Father said *not* to do.

When Father arrived, should she tell him about Ben? Felicity sighed. She wished she could tell Father. But she had made a promise to Ben, and she

knew she had to keep it. Felicity took a piece of
paper out of her pocketbook. She began to draw a
map of the route from Grandfather's plantation to
Yorktown. She would help Ben run away, even
though she did not want him to go.

Felicity held her pocketbook to her chest as she
ran to the woods. A storm was coming. The wind
was fitful, and the air was yellowish green. Her
hair was wild and she was out of breath when she
reached Ben. "Ben!" she said. "Father is coming.
He's put a notice in the *Gazette* about you and
offered a reward for your return. Will you stay and

talk to him?"

"No," said Ben, just as Felicity had expected.

"Then you had better leave right away," said Felicity. "Come, stand up and follow me. I'll show you the path to Yorktown. Hurry."

Ben said not a word as he stood up. He winced as he put his weight on his injured leg, and he wobbled a bit when he tried to walk.

"Here," said Felicity. "Lean on me. You can do it."

Felicity supported Ben as they made their way through the woods along the footpath. She and Grandfather had ridden along the path many times, so Felicity was sure of the way. But she and Ben moved very slowly. The path was narrow, and bumpy with tree roots. Ben struggled and stumbled. It felt like hours before they reached Philgate's Creek. Felicity helped Ben across, wading through the shallow water. They rested a minute on the far shore. Then Felicity handed Ben her pocketbook.

"I'm going back now," she said. "Take this. There's a map inside to show you the rest of the way to Yorktown. And I've put money in it, too.

It's not much, but it should pay your
fare on the ferry to Gloucester. Be
sure to follow my map. Stay on
the path. Don't take the main road
or . . ." Felicity hesitated, "or there may
be trouble."

Ben nodded. "Good-bye, Lissie," he said.
"Thank you. I won't forget you."

Felicity was too sad to speak. She watched
Ben's back until it disappeared, swallowed up in
the mouth of a leafy tunnel. She wondered if she'd
ever see Ben again. A fat raindrop hit her shoulder,
and she turned to go.

It was almost noon and the rain was steady
when Felicity got back to the house. As she came
inside, Felicity heard unfamiliar voices in the parlor.
Probably guests for dinner, she thought. She began to
go up the stairs to her chamber. She stopped dead
still when she heard one of the voices say, "Don't
you worry, sir. We'll find the apprentice lad and
bring him back if we have to drag him!"

Felicity sat down hard. Another voice, even
rougher than the first one, said, "As soon as we
saw Mr. Merriman's notice, my partner and me, we

*"Don't you worry, sir. We'll find the apprentice lad and bring
him back if we have to drag him!"*

didn't waste no time. We set out to find the run-
away."

"Well, I can assure you the lad is not anywhere
on my plantation," said Grandfather. "Someone
would have seen him."

"All right, sir. If you say so, sir," said the first
man. "We'll be on our way to Yorktown then. We'll
ask at the ferry if he went across the river to
Gloucester. If he did, we'll follow him."

The ferry! thought Felicity in a panic. That was
exactly where Ben was headed! If they left now, and
took the main road, these men would get to the
ferry before Ben would. Ben would walk straight
into a trap!

"We've dealt with runaways before, sir," the
second man was saying. "We ain't afraid to be
rough if needs be."

Felicity did not hear what Grandfather replied.
She was up and away, out the door, running to the
stable through the rain. She had to stop Ben. She
had to find him before those men did.

PENNY SAVES
THE DAY

Felicity did not stop to saddle Penny. She slipped the bridle over Penny's head, led her from the stable, climbed up on the pasture fence, and swung herself onto Penny's back. Then she leaned forward and whispered to Penny, "This is not going to be easy, Penny my girl. The footpath will be slippery in this rain. But you must help me find Ben. I know we can do it."

The storm grew angrier and the rain fell harder as Penny carried Felicity into the woods. Wet branches waved around them wildly. They looked like long green arms warning *turn back! turn back!* Felicity was blinded by the rain. She leaned low over Penny's neck and trusted Penny to find the way. Penny never faltered. Thunder crashed, making Felicity's heart jump. Lightning ripped the sky with sharp, wicked slashes. Through it all, Penny kept on in an easy canter, though the path was slick. Felicity knew Penny sensed her fear and urgency, but Penny was calm. It was as if she had turned all her willfulness and spirit to one task: helping Felicity find Ben.

When they came to Philgate's Creek, Penny jumped over the churning water in one smooth arch. Felicity whispered to her, "That's my girl. That's my Penny." Then on through the rain they rode.

Just past the turnoff for Sandy Point, Penny slowed. Felicity looked up and saw Ben scrambling into the woods, trying to hide.

"Ben! Stop!" she cried. "It's me!"

Ben turned. "Felicity!" he gasped, as Penny came toward him. "Why are you here?"

"Listen to me, Ben," said Felicity. She took a deep breath and then spilled the whole story in a rush. "When I got back to Grandfather's, two men were there. They had seen Father's notice in the newspaper. They are after you for the reward. They said they'd be rough with you, and I believe them. They are on their way to Yorktown now. They are going straight to the ferry, so they would be sure to catch you and probably beat you and drag you back." Felicity leaned toward Ben. "Can't you see how dangerous and foolish this running away is, Ben? Wouldn't you rather face Father than those two men? Come back with me now. Come back. Please."

Ben shook his head. "I can't," he said. "That would be cowardly."

Felicity was furious. She said just what she thought Grandfather would say. "You *are* a coward, Ben Davidson," she said. "It's cowardly to run away, to break promises, and to hurt those who need you and trust you. Now, will you come back?"

Ben was quiet. He put his hand on Penny's neck. She did not shy away. Then Ben said, "Will Penny let me ride her?"

Felicity smiled. "She will if I ask her to," she said.

"You are a coward, Ben Davidson," Felicity said.

"Indeed," Ben grinned. "It is hard to refuse you, Felicity Merriman."

The wind had calmed and the rain was falling more gently as Penny carried Felicity and Ben back through the woods. It was as if the storm had worn itself out with its fury and was now tired and weepy. Felicity was tired, too. She thought Penny must be, as well, though the horse walked on at a steady pace. Felicity patted Penny's neck. What a fine, brave horse she was!

Felicity had to leave behind her tiredness and gather all the bravery she could muster when she led Ben into the parlor to face Mother and Grandfather. Grandfather's face went white with anger when he saw Ben. His gray eyes were hard as gunmetal. He said nothing.

But Mother stood and smiled a small smile. "Ben," she said. "I am so glad you have . . . I am so glad you are here."

"Ben has decided not to run away," said Felicity. "He has been hiding in the woods by the river. I've been . . . I've been helping him. I'm sorry. I knew it was wrong, but I had to. Today I showed him the footpath to Yorktown. But then those men came, and I was afraid they would hurt Ben. So I followed him and . . . and . . ."

Ben spoke up. "Felicity convinced me not to go," he said. "She brought me back." He glanced at Grandfather and then said to Mother, "I am very sorry I ran away."

"Aye, indeed," said Mother quickly. "We will have time enough for apologies when Mr. Merriman comes. But now I daresay 'twould be best for both of you to find dry clothes. Come with me."

They were almost out the door when Grandfather called, "Felicity!"

Felicity turned around. "Yes, Grandfather?" she said softly.

"The lad says 'twas you who convinced him to come back," said Grandfather. "I am curious. How did you do it?"

"Well," said Felicity. She thought back over the things she had said to Ben. Then she remembered what had convinced him to change his mind. "I just said to him exactly what I thought *you* would have said, Grandfather."

"Humph!" said Grandfather. "Did you indeed?"

He almost smiled. "Go along, then," he said. "You're as wet as if you'd jumped into the river."

After an early supper, Felicity went to her bedchamber. She lay in bed listening to the night music the crickets and frogs made.  A warm wind blew the soothing murmur of the river up to her. The storm that day had been violent, but like most violent storms, it was short. It left the air washed clean and sweet. Felicity fell asleep, worn out by her adventures.

When Father arrived in the morning, Felicity was at breakfast. Ben was still asleep, and Mother said not to wake him. So Felicity led Father to the stable to visit Penny.

"Father," Felicity said, "I was wrong to help Ben run away and not to tell anybody. And I am sorry. But I had to keep his secret." She stroked Penny's neck. "Because Ben kept my secret about Penny last autumn."

"I understand," said Father. He looked at Penny. "Penny is a beautiful horse. You're glad to have her back, aren't you, Lissie?"

"Aye," said Felicity. She hugged Penny. "And I am glad she is safe from the likes of Mr. Nye."

"Everyone is safe from Jiggy Nye for the present," said Father. "When I left Williamsburg, Jiggy Nye was in jail." Father looked at Felicity. "You'll miss Penny when you leave here to go back to Williamsburg, won't you?"

"Aye," said Felicity again, slowly. "But it won't be as bad as it was before, when I helped Penny run away and I didn't know whether I'd ever see her again. I know where she is now."

"You know she's safe," agreed Father. "Maybe that will make it a little easier to say good-bye. But," he sighed, "I'm afraid it's never very easy to say good-bye to friends we love."

"No," said Felicity. "But sometimes saying good-bye isn't the end of a friendship. I said good-bye to Penny when I let her go, but she came back."

"That she did," agreed Father.

Felicity looked at him very seriously. "I've been thinking about Ben," she said. "You could let him go be a soldier, Father. The fighting won't last forever. You could trust Ben to come

55

back to you when the fighting is over. I know you could trust him."

Father did not answer, but Felicity knew he was thinking about what she had said.

In a little while, Ben appeared in the doorway of the stable. "I have come to apologize, Mr. Merriman," said Ben. "I'm sorry. 'Twas wrong to run away. I meant no disrespect to you, sir. You have always treated me well and fairly. But . . ." Ben squared his shoulders. "I do want to be a soldier."

Mr. Merriman stared at Ben for a while. Then he said, "Ben, I will not allow you to break your apprenticeship agreement with me. You are but sixteen. You are pledged to me for three more years. I expect you to give me three more years of service."

Ben nodded sadly.

Mr. Merriman went on slowly. "But in a little more than a year, you will be eighteen. If at that time you still wish to be a soldier, and if there is still such a thing as the Patriots' army, then I will let you go. But we must have the understanding that you will come back and finish out your service to me when your days of being a soldier are over. Does that seem fair to you?"

Ben's face brightened. "Yes, sir," he said. "Thank you, sir."

Father smiled at Felicity, and then turned to shake Ben's hand. "Good lad," he said. "I know that I can trust you."

"Aye, sir," said Ben. "You can."

All too soon, the sad day came when Felicity and her family had to return to Williamsburg. That last morning, Felicity and Grandfather rode out to see the sunrise together one more time. Felicity watched a branch bobbing along in the river. It sailed by, carried on the current, and soon disappeared from sight on its way to the sea. Grandfather watched it, too.

"Felicity," Grandfather said, "the world is changing. 'Tis changing too fast for an old man like me to keep up with it." He smiled at Felicity. "But how can I mind growing older, when I can watch you growing up, becoming a fine young lady, full of strength and wisdom and love."

Then Grandfather chuckled. "Indeed, many things are too fast for an old man like me," he said. "Especially that horse of yours. What am I to do with such a fast horse? I can't catch her, and she wouldn't let me ride her even if I could catch her. I think you had better take Penny back to Williamsburg with you. Your father tells me that Jiggy Nye is in jail, so she will be safe. Will you take good care of Penny for me?"

"Oh, yes, Grandfather!" exclaimed Felicity. "Thank you! I will! Oh, I truly will." Felicity was trembling, she was so happy.

"Very well, then," said Grandfather. He gathered up his reins. "Come along. You've a great deal to say good-bye to this morning."

Felicity gave Penny a quick hug. Then she gathered her reins, too, and followed Grandfather to the fields. The plantation had never looked more lovely. But Felicity could think about only one thing: *Penny was going home with her!*

After breakfast, there were many hugs, kisses, thank-you's and good-bye's. Then Mother, Nan, Ben, and William climbed into the carriage. Father and Felicity rode beside them on their horses. Felicity sat tall and proud on Penny's back. She wished she could gallop all the way back to Williamsburg. She couldn't wait to show Penny to Elizabeth. But just as they reached the end of the lane, Felicity stopped. She turned around and looked back. Grandfather was standing on the steps of his house, his arm still raised to wave farewell. He looked very small, almost lost in the shadows of the trees.

"Wait for me, Father," said Felicity. She urged Penny into a fast canter and rode back to Grandfather. When she reached him, Felicity jumped off Penny and ran to give Grandfather one last hug.

Felicity climbed back on Penny and hurried to join her family. She felt a sweet sadness at leaving Grandfather and this place that was so dear to her. But she rode on, into the sunshine ahead.

LOOKING
BACK
1·7·7·4

A PEEK INTO
THE PAST

*Plantation owners built their homes on the highest point of land to
look important. Other buildings, like the kitchen, dairy, and smokehouse,
were built on lower ground.*

For at least half the year, Virginia sizzles with heat.
Today, families may take vacations to the mountains or
places in the North to escape the steamy, sticky weather.
But back in colonial times, roads were poor and travel
was difficult. People seldom went on trips, and women
and children traveled even less than men. When families
did travel, they visited friends and relatives, and often
stayed for weeks at a time.

For a girl like Felicity growing up in town, visits to

relatives in the country were great fun. Felicity's grandfather lived on a large farm, or *plantation*. There Felicity could play with farm animals, take walks through the gardens and orchards, and watch boats on the river nearby. Her family enjoyed barbecues, fish fries, and other picnics during the warm summer days. Felicity and other children loved to go horseback riding and fishing, too.

The eighteenth-century children in this drawing are playing on a handmade seesaw.

Since there was no electricity in Felicity's day, there were no fans or air conditioners. Colonists in both town and country had to find other ways to stay cool. Homes often had high ceilings and a wide central hallway that stretched between the front and back doors. People sat in this hallway and even ate their meals there during summer months because the open doors at each end let the breeze blow through.

Many people put Venetian blinds or shutters on their windows and closed them during the day to keep out the hot sun. On windy days and during the evenings, the windows and shutters or blinds could be opened to let in a refreshing breeze. To keep the house cool, the kitchen—where a fire often burned all day—was a separate building, usually located behind the house.

This colonial girl kept the sun off her face with a wide-brimmed hat. Children's clothing was just beginning to be less restricting.

Colonists wore lighter clothing in the summer, though girls and women still wore ankle-length gowns, and nobody wore shorts! Boys cooled off by finding a place to swim, but it was not proper for girls to go swimming. People used hand-held fans to cool themselves, and girls and women wore wide-brimmed hats to keep the hot sun off their faces when they worked or strolled in their gardens.

All Virginia plantations had large gardens. They provided fruits and vegetables to eat, and flowers to delight the eye. The gardens were always kept neat and attractive because the plantation owner's family and their visitors often walked in the gardens for pleasure and exercise.

Virginia colonists grew most of the same fruits and vegetables that gardeners do today. Herbs were used in cooking and in medicine.

For example, one recipe for a toothache called for putting juice from an herb called *rue* into the patient's ear on the same side as the aching tooth. Some herbal remedies really did help, but others did nothing, or even made the illness worse!

In eastern Virginia where Grandfather lived in the 1770s, grains such as wheat and corn were the major crops. While small farms were usually run by the farmer and his family alone, plantations depended on slaves. Slaves planted, tended, and harvested the crops. The owner of a plantation, who was called the *planter*, might have a few to 100 slaves, depending on the size of his plantation.

Planters provided slave families with small one-room cabins, simple clothing, and corn to fix in many

Eighteenth-century books about plants included beautiful drawings of flowers.

ways for food. Most slaves worked in the fields from sunup to sundown. Some slaves learned skills like shoemaking, carpentry, or weaving. That way, the plantation could provide many things it needed from the work of its slaves. A

Slaves sometimes enjoyed music and danced during their little free time. This drum was made by a Virginia slave in the 1700s.

few slaves worked in the main house and did the cooking, cleaning, and child care for the planter's family.

Slaves had little time to themselves. On Sundays and holidays, slaves tended small gardens of their own and spent time with their families. Telling stories, singing, and dancing helped them enjoy at least part of their lives, which were directed by the slave owner in every other way. Some owners treated their slaves very harshly, and any planter could separate slave families by selling off husbands, wives, or children.

A white overseer, or supervisor hired by the plantation owner, watches two slave women hard at work.

Many slaves tried to escape, and some succeeded. A few slaves saved enough money over time to buy their freedom. Others fought in the Revolutionary War and were given their freedom afterward.

The war had just started during the summer Felicity was ten. In Virginia, men were beginning to sign up to fight in the war. Slaves had not yet been asked to join the fight for independence. Life on plantations like Grandfather's continued as it had in earlier years, though people worried about how the war would change their lives.

A poster urging Patriots to join the new army.

67